LITTLE CASTLES OF BOHEMIA

GERARD
LA·BRVNIE

GÉRARD DE NERVAL

LITTLE CASTLES OF BOHEMIA

PROSE AND POETRY

Illustrations by Alfred Prunaire

Translated by Napoleon Jeffries

WAKEFIELD PRESS

CAMBRIDGE, MASSACHUSETTS

Wakefield Press, P.O. Box 425645, Cambridge, MA 02142

Originally published as *Petits châteaux de Bohême: Prose et poésie* in 1853.

This book was set in Minion Pro and Myriad Pro by Wakefield Press. Printed and bound by Versa Press in the United States of America.

ISBN: 978-1-962728-08-9

Available through D.A.P./Distributed Art Publishers
75 Broad Street, Suite 630
New York, New York 10004
Tel: (212) 627-1999
Fax: (212) 627-9484

10 9 8 7 6 5 4 3 2 1

CONTENTS

SECOND CASTLE

THIRD CASTLE

MYSTICISM

LYRICISM

TRANSLATOR'S INTRODUCTION

Although Gérard de Nerval had originally intended it to be a small anthology of his early poetry, *Little Castles of Bohemia* ended up as something more. As could be said of all his last works, this book was an effort at stability: worn out from his travels and spells of mental turmoil, and financially impoverished, Nerval gathered his past writing, here and in the prose collection *Les Filles du Feu* (Daughters of fire), in an attempt at assembling some sort of posterity, at creating a home for these vagabond pieces.

The title of this book reflects the ending of one of his last works, the melancholic *Walks and Memories*. At the close of that divagating autobiographical narrative, Nerval takes refuge from a rain shower with a family of entertainers in their traveling carriage. Fatigued by his lengthy perambulations through the towns and memories of his youth, in search of a home as well as some coherence to the life he had lived, he momentarily entertains the idea of staying in that "wandering house." It is a momentary whim, but a solution nonetheless to those years in which Haussmann was razing and rebuilding Paris; years in which Nerval, after the razing brought on by his sojourn in the "devil's castle," was trying to rebuild his life.

Nerval borrowed this idea of a Bohemian castle—a rootless edifice and wandering refuge—from his friend, Charles Nodier, who in his 1830 Laurence Sterne–inspired *Histoire du*

roi de Bohême et de ses sept chateaux declared there to be seven such castles in a man's life. Nerval limits them to three—youth, love, and despair—and in the present collection they take on the forms of the classic allegorical seasons.

The first castle, naturally enough, is that of spring. The usual themes are to be found therein: love, youth, friendship, ideals, and enthusiasm. The poems themselves are appropriately slight, charming but green with youth (although among them are two acknowledged classics, "Fantasia" and "The Cydalises"). Most of what they hold, though, are already geared toward, and dwell on, the colder spell of loss and disillusionment to come—"gloomy chords" which the autobiographical reminiscences help to accentuate. These poems are remnants, and this debris of Nerval's past—memories preserved in the paintings and paneling he rescues from the demolition workers of the first castle—will be regathered in his room in the asylum of his later years, as poignantly described toward the end of his memoir of madness, *Aurélia*.

These reminiscences of the first castle eventually transition to the second castle: ambition, coupled with his embracement of the ideal, forces Nerval to abandon the "prey for the shadow"—that is, to abandon the realizable love of spring for the theatrical love of summer. *Corilla* is better known for its inclusion in *Les filles du feu*, where it follows "Octavie" and "Isis" to form Nerval's Neapolitan triad.[1] But though their settings are the same, the differences between *Corilla* and "Octavie" reveal the point of interest, for the two are inverted mirrors of each other: the theatricized autobiography of "Octavie" becomes autobiographical theater in *Corilla*. The various facets to Nerval's syncretic love interests are all present in the figure of Corilla, who embodies both the "easy conquest" of the seamstress in "Octavie," as well as that same story's idealized (and significantly absent) prima donna. "Octavie" contains, of course, a third and more complicated woman—Octavie herself, who could be seen as representing the potential unification of both reality and ideal. This personification of the water sprite, a "daughter of the waters" who can mingle with both the fires of Mount Vesuvius and the burning footlights of the theater, also finds expression in the figure of Corilla, who manages to flit at will from the (illusory) ideal of the prima donna to the (illusory) reality of the flower seller. She is ultimately neither, as she refuses (as Aurélie does in "Sylvie") the idealized role of the first and employs the second only as a ruse: she is a woman who refuses to fit into the projections of her admirers (who admire what they want to see, not who she is).

But by reducing both reality and the ideal to roles to be performed, Nerval's ambition, as stated in the first castle, is fulfilled—namely, to "reunite in a stroke of fire the two halves of [his] double love." Doing so, though, seems to necessitate dividing himself in two. The cynical Don Juan and the romantic idealist, roles that Nerval carried out (to his dissatisfaction) in "Octavie," are here separate characters. "Every man has a double," Nerval says in *Aurélia*: "In everyone is a spectator and an actor." In *Aurélia*, Nerval is a spectator, forced to watch his double marry his love in a mystical wedding. Here, he and his other, in the characters of Fabio and Marcelli, are in equal conflict, but are ultimately reconciled in their shared failure to fully win Corilla's heart. The tragedy of "Octavie" and *Aurélia*, then, is tempered here, both in this reconciliation and in the fact that our two heroes are almost buffoons: one has to wonder at Corilla's interest in either—even if her own interest perhaps lies in the two of them together, dreamer and realist united in one love.

For this reason, the shift to the third castle may seem somewhat disjointed without a reference to Nerval's better-known works. In a sense, his third castle can be seen as the domain of resignation: the leaving or loss of the stage. This leaving or loss goes beyond the typical melancholy of autumnal old age and the waning of one's forces, though: given the context of Nerval's late autobiographical works, we know this third castle also encompassed a leave of reason and a journey into the depths of despair.

A moment in *Corilla* hints at the darkness lying in wait for the romantic dreamer: the cynical Marcelli remarks that when he had come upon Fabio, the latter was on the verge of throwing himself over *la rampe*—which is to say, over the handrail and into the water to drown himself. While Marcelli is mistaken as to Fabio's suicidal intentions, it is worth noting that *la rampe* can also refer to the footlights of a stage, setting up a metaphorical parallel between the passage from life to death and that from stage to audience (and vice versa). Fabio's actions in the play are indeed his attempt at walking onto the stage of his ideal and embracing the love he has assembled in his mind. Doing so, of course, forces his ideal to leave the stage for reality and set a new stage for disappointment.

If the fourth castle, and the winter and death it embodies, remains absent, the threat of madness and the abyss of existential despair can nonetheless be descried, particularly in the devastating sonnet cycle "Christ in the Olive Grove." Nerval here adapts and develops Jean Paul's famous "Speech of the Dead Christ from the Universe That There Is No God" from his eccentrically titled novel *Flower-, Fruit-, and Thornpieces; or, The Married Life, Death, and Wedding of Advocate of the Poor F. St. Siebenkäs.*[2] But where in Jean Paul's novel the character Siebenkäs awakens from his nightmare of a godless universe to worship anew with a soul weeping with joy, Nerval's ruminating verses on the death of God point to no such awakening. A syncretic universe as described in the "Golden Verses" that follows, in which all of nature is imbued with God or Goddess, plays at the footlights of an abyss, no less dark for being staged.

The threat of madness and despair—what Nerval titles "Mysticism" in his third castle—concludes almost anticlimactically with an Orphic look backward to the theater in the final short section "Lyricism." This last section consists of light verse, some of it remnants of the planned opera of the first castle: these lyrical ruins of songs that were never sung essentially cast a silent last glance at the "adored features of the past." A calm after the storm of mysticism, in which the edifice Nerval proposed for this collection seemed to all but collapse into shapeless, existential despair.

*

But a less autobiographical approach to this book can be taken, for *Little Castles of Bohemia* also serves as a general portrait of the nineteenth-century Bohemian. As Joanna Richardson states at the opening of her book on the lineage of the French Bohemian, "The first Bohemians were the young Romantics in the Impasse du Doyenné in the early 1830s," and the happy youth Nerval presents here is a first-person snapshot of the culture that would cultivate Charles Baudelaire, Jules-Amédée Barbey d'Aurevilly, and Paul Verlaine in later Parisian locales.[3] Concluding one's life in misery and madness constituted more of a norm than an exception in the lives of the Bohemians, and if Nerval's life and work stand out from those of many of his contemporaries, it is due more to the degree of his talent than to his tragedy, and is why he is read more today than such poets as Charles Babara, Étienne Eggis, or Philoxène Boyer, whose lives didn't lack for miserable conclusions.

For the almost inevitable tragedy to the Bohemian life was, in retrospect, part and parcel of its philosophy. As Nerval's contemporary, Alexandre Guyard de Saint-Chéron, wrote in the pages of *L'Artiste* (in which much of the present book had originally been published), the artist "must no longer divide his life into two separate parts, that of the artist and that of the private individual. He must live an undivided life, have an undivided inspiration."[4] The theme of doubling, division, and what would prove to be impossible unification belonged as much to the Bohemian life as it did Nerval's own journey through the stations of these castles. Bohemia lay at the root of Nerval's later madness, which consisted of the doubling of himself and his love, and the impossibility of reconciling these doubles—of reconciling reality with the ideal described by art. If Nerval claimed the poet's life to be structurally that of "everyone," the Bohemian's life injected it with an intensity difficult to bear at length.

The collapse of the boundary between art and life was one modern aspect to Bohemia, but the mixture of poetry, prose, and theater in *Little Castles of Bohemia* also makes for a modern work, and their arrangement casts light on how Nerval regarded these genres. By Nerval's account, poetry "falls" into prose, an indication that his repeated claims of being only a "humble writer of prose" positioned him as a literary Icarus, a writer who considered himself to have fallen from grace.[5] Since Nerval is best remembered for his final works of prose and the late sonnet-cycle "Les Chimères," a reader today may feel puzzled at this self assessment, given the triviality of many of his early *odelettes*. When he first introduced the "Chimères," Nerval had asked, in a note to Alexandre Dumas, to "at least give me credit for [their] expression." Such humility over the sonnets, now recognized as being among the greatest French poems of the nineteenth century, was certainly unwarranted and seems like an apology that would bear more relation to his early verse.

What should be kept in mind, though, is that Nerval considered his early poems to be not so much "works" as, rather, *vessels*—poems to be not read but sung. Poetry as conceived in Nerval's first castle was to be filled and fulfilled by the singer—the embodiment of the ideal—the way the banal verses of Corilla's "Italian Air" transform her from a flower girl into a "veritable" goddess. Poetry for Nerval was form: not the words of an oracle, but rather a veil to cover Isis. The theater was his attempt at poetry's realization, a temple in which women became goddesses. The prose that ultimately followed in works such as *Aurelia* and *Les filles de feu* was in some ways a reflection on his failure in both genres—a failure, however, that enabled the realization of those final masterpieces. In our own days of collapse, Nerval's castles are to be explored as much for their fault lines as for their construction.

✶

This translation follows Jean-Luc Steinmetz's presentation and arrangement of *Petits châteaux de Bohême* in the Pléiade edition of Nerval's *Œuvres complètes*, volume III (Paris: Éditions Gallimard, 1993). Much of the information to be found in the endnotes comes from his annotations, which have also informed this introduction. I also owe a debt to George MacLennan, whose reading saved me from a number of blunders and helped move this translation from the clutches of my own days of green youth into its final version. Any fault to be found with this translation of course remains my own.

NOTES

1. Translations of both "Octavie" and "Isis," along with *Walks and Memories*, can be found in *Aurélia & Other Writings* (Cambridge, MA: Exact Change, 1996).
2. Sections II and III of Nerval's sequence are direct reworkings of the dreamt Christ's words in Jean Paul's novel: see *Jean Paul: A Reader*, ed. Timothy J. Casey, trans. Erika Casey (Baltimore: Johns Hopkins University Press, 1992), 182.
3. Joanna Richardson, *The Bohemians: La Vie de Boheme in Paris 1830–1914* (South Brunswick and New York: A.S. Barnes, 1971), 11. Readers wanting a more fleshed-out account in English of the Impasse du Doyenné can consult the chapter she devotes to it in that book.
4. Richardson, *The Bohemians*, 22.
5. An attitude not unique to Nerval: his friend, the poet Théophile Gautier, who plays a role in these pages, portrayed a similar fall in his poem "Adieu à la poésie" (Farewell to Poetry): "Come fallen angel, and your pink wings close; / Doff your white robe, your rays that gild the skies; / You must—from heaven, where once you used to rise—Streak, like a shooting star, fall into prose" (trans. Norman R. Shapiro in *Selected Lyrics* by Théophile Gautier [New Haven: Yale University Press, 2010], 353).

LITTLE CASTLES OF BOHEMIA

TO A FRIEND

O primavera, gioventù dell'anno,
Bella madre di fiori,
D'erbe novelle e di novelli amori . . .
Pastor Fido[1]

My friend,[2] you asked me if I could dig up some of my old verse, and you even inquired as to the manner of poet I used to be, long before I became a humble writer of prose.

I send you the three ages of the poet—there remains in me nothing more than an obstinate writer of prose. I wrote the first verses in the enthusiasm of youth, the second in love, and the last in despair. The Muse entered my heart like a goddess with golden words; she escaped from it like a prophetess letting out screams of pain. Yet her last accents softened as she grew distant. She turned back a moment, and I saw again, as in a mirage, those adored features of the past!

The poet's life is that of everyone. I see no point in defining all its stages. And now:

Let us build, once again, this ruined castle my friend
Which the breath of the world has flung down to the sand,
And put back the sofa by the Flemish paintings . . .[3]

FIRST CASTLE

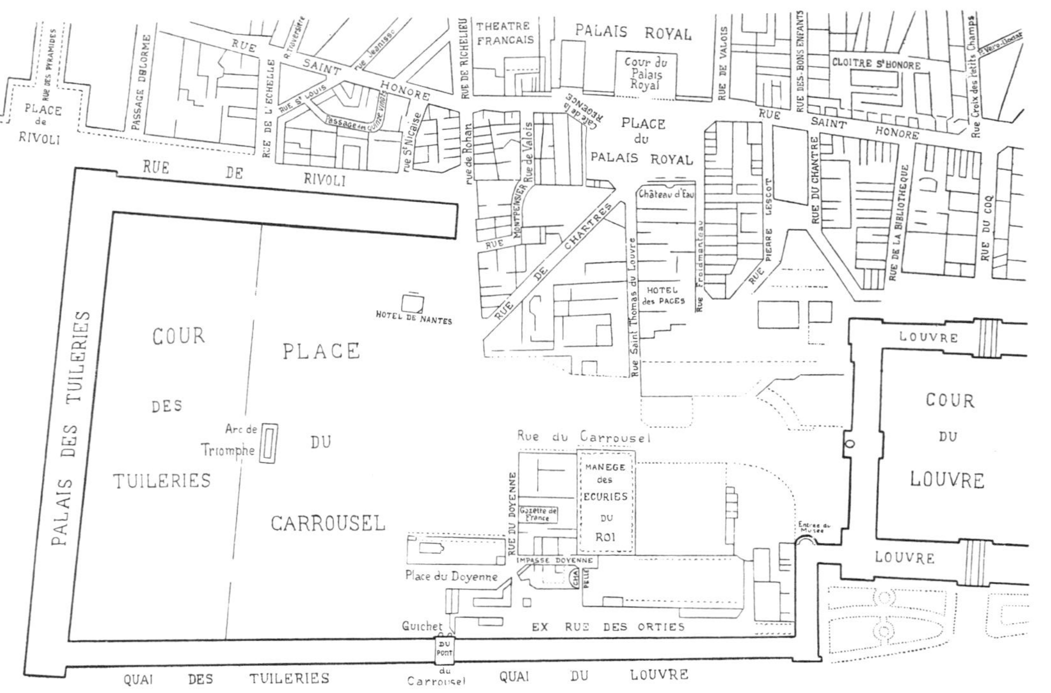
PLACE de RIVOLI
RUE DES PYRAMIDES
PASSAGE DELORME
RUE SAINT HONORE
R. Traversière
rue Jeanisson
RUE DE L'ECHELLE
RUE St LOUIS
Passage des Quinze vingts
rue St Nicaise
RUE DE RIVOLI
RUE DE RICHELIEU
rue de Rohan
THEATRE FRANCAIS
PALAIS ROYAL
Cour du Palais Royal
Café de la Régence
PLACE du PALAIS ROYAL
Rue de Valois
RUE MONTPENSIER
RUE DE CHARTRES
Château d'Eau
Rue Saint Thomas du Louvre
HOTEL des PAGES
Rue Froidmanteau
RUE DE VALOIS
RUE DES BONS ENFANTS
CLOITRE St HONORE
Rue Croix des Petits Champs
RUE PIERRE LESCOT
RUE DU CHANTRE
RUE DE LA BIBLIOTHEQUE
RUE DU COQ
HOTEL DE NANTES
LOUVRE
COUR DU LOUVRE
LOUVRE
PALAIS DES TUILERIES
COUR DES TUILERIES
PLACE DU CARROUSEL
Arc de Triomphe
Rue du Carrousel
MANEGE des ECURIES DU ROI
RUE DU DOYENNE
Gazette de France
IMPASSE DOYENNE
Place du Doyenne
CHA PELLE
Entrée du Musée
Guichet
DU PONT du Carrousel
EX RUE DES ORTIES
QUAI DES TUILERIES
QUAI DU LOUVRE

I

RUE DU DOYENNÉ

It was in our shared lodgings on rue du Doyenné[4] that we recognized each other as brothers—*Arcades ambo*[5]—in a corner of the old Louvre of the Médicis—very near where the Hôtel de Rambouillet used to stand.

The dean's old salon, with its four double doors and its ceiling historiated with rocaille and guivres—restored through the care of so many painters, our friends, who have since become famous—echoed with our gallant rhymes, often punctuated by the joyous laughter or mad songs of the Cydalises.

Good old Rogier[6] was smiling in his beard atop a ladder, where he was painting a Neptune on one of the three glass coverings—who looked like himself! Then the double doors opened with a crash: it was Théophile.[7]—We bustled about to offer him a Louis XIII armchair, and he read, in turn, his first verses—while Cydalise I, or Lorry, or Victorine, swung nonchalantly in Sarah the blonde's hammock, which was stretched across the enormous salon.[8]

Sometimes one of us would stand and dream up new verses by the windows while gazing at the sculpted façades of the Museum's gallery, enlivened on our side by the trees of the riding school.

You said it well:

Théo, do you recall those seasons green as poems
Which so quickly would shed their leaves in those old homes,
Whose fronts would take cover by a wing of the Louvre?[9]

Or else, through the facing windows, which looked onto the cul-de-sac, we would direct vague provocations to the Spanish eyes of the commissioner's wife, who often appeared above the municipal streetlight.

What happy times! We gave dances, dinners, fancy parties—we put on old comedies, and Mademoiselle Plessy,[10] still a debutant actress in those days, agreed to take on a role for one of them:—it was that of Béatrice in *Jodelet*.[11] And how comical our poor Édouard[12] was in the roles of Harlequin!*

We were young, always gay, often wealthy . . . But I've just struck a gloomy chord: our palace is razed to the ground. I trampled through its debris this past autumn. Even the ruins of the chapel, which stood out so gracefully against the green of the trees—and whose dome had one day collapsed in the eighteenth century on six unfortunate canons gathered to perform a service—has not been respected. The day when they cut down the trees of the riding school, I will go there to read again Ronsard's *Felled Forest*:

Listen to me, woodsman, rest your arm, take it slow:
These are not merely trees which you are laying low;
See you not everywhere the blood, dripping and dark,
Of all the nymphs who lived beneath the hardened bark?

That ends like this, as you know:

---

* Particularly in the *Courier of Naples*, at the théâtre des grands boulevards.

Matter always remains whereas form disappears!

It was around then that I found myself, once again, wealthy enough to repurchase and carry away from the demolition workers two lots of paneling from the salon, painted by our friends. I have the two top panels of Nanteuil's door;[13] Wattier's *Watteau*, signed;[14] Corot's two long panels, depicting two Provence *Landscapes*; Châtillon's *Red Monk*,[15]

reading the Bible on the arched hip of a nude woman, asleep;* the *Bacchantes*, by Chassériau,[16] who have tigers on a leash as if they were dogs; Rogier's two overmantels, in which the Cydalise, in Regency costume, a taffeta dress the color of dead leaves—sad omen—smiles with her Chinese eyes as she inhales a rose before the full-length portrait of Théophile dressed as a Spaniard. The *horrid* landlord—who lived on the ground floor, but on whose head we too often danced—after the two years of suffering which had led him to give us notice, covered all those paintings with a coating of tempera because, he claimed, the nudity prevented him from renting to bourgeois.—I thank God he was thrifty enough not to use oil paint.

* Same subject as the painting at Victor Hugo's.

So, all of that is more or less saved. I have not recovered Lorentz's *Siege of Lérida*,[17] in which the French army launches an attack, preceded by violins; nor the two little *Landscapes* by Rousseau, which someone will have no doubt cut out in advance;[18] but I have, by Lorentz, a powdered *marshal*, in Louis XV uniform.—As for the Renaissance bed, the Medici console, the two sideboards,* the *Ribeira*,† the tapestries of the *Four Elements*—all of that was scattered a long time ago. "Where did you lose so many beautiful things?" Balzac asked me one day.—"In misfortune!" I replied, citing one of his favorite words.

* Fortunately, Alphonse Karr owns the sideboard with the three women and the three satyrs, with oval paintings of the time on the doors.[19]

† The *Death of Saint Joseph* is in London, at Gavarni's.[20]

II

PORTRAITS

Let us speak again of the Cydalise, or rather, let us say but a word:—She is forever embalmed and preserved in the pure crystal of a sonnet by Théophile[21]—by Théo, as we used to call him.

Théophile always looked like a robust man; he never grew a paunch, though, and has kept himself as we knew him. Our skimpy clothes are so absurd that Antinous, dressed in tails, would seem enormous, as would Venus in a modern dress: the former would look like a market porter in his Sunday best, the latter like a fishmonger. Our friend's colossal frame (we can say as much, since he is traveling in Greece right now) was often to his detriment with ladies subscribing to fashion magazines; a more perfect knowledge maintained the favor of the weaker and more intelligent sex; he enjoyed a great reputation in our circle and was not always dying at the Chinese feet of the Cydalise.

Going further back in my memories, I find a skinny Théophile . . . You did not know him. I saw him one day, stretched out on a bed—long and green—chest laden with cupping glasses. He was slowly on his way to rejoining his pseudonym, Théophile de Viau, whose pantheistic loves you have described—along the shadowy path of *Sylvie's Lane*.[22] Those two poets, separated by two centuries, would have shaken hands far too soon in Virgil's Elysian Fields.

This is what happened:

There were several of us, friends of an earlier society,[23] gaily leading a life that was in fashion those days, even for serious people. This dying Théophile was distressing us and we had some new ideas concerning hygienics, which we conveyed to his parents. The parents understood, something rather uncommon; but they loved their son. The doctor was dismissed, and we said to Théo: "Get up . . . and have supper."[24] The weakness of his stomach worried us more than anything. He had fallen asleep and felt ill at the first performance of *Robert le Diable*.[25]

The doctor was called back. He began to reflect and, seeing him full of health on waking, told the parents: "His friends may be right."

After that, Théophile flourished.—There was no more talk of cupping glasses, and he was handed over to us. Nature had made him a poet; our care made him nearly immortal. What had the most impact on his constitution was a certain preparation of blackcurrant liqueur without sugar, which his sisters served him in enormous sandstone amphoras from the Beauvais factory; Ziégler has since given whimsical forms to what until then had been but simple big-bellied pitchers.[26] When we communicated our poetic inspirations, we took the precaution of covering the bedroom with padding so that the *paroxysm*, sometimes due to the Bacchus of the blackcurrant liqueur, did not harm our heads with the angles of the furniture.

Once Théophile was saved, he started drinking nothing but red wine mixed with water and a drop of champagne with light suppers.

III

THE QUEEN OF SHEBA

Let us go back.—We had given up all hope of beguiling the commissioner's wife.—Her husband, less timid than her, had answered, with a most polite letter, the collective invitation we had addressed to them. As it was impossible to sleep in those old houses owing to the choreographic results of our suppers—furnished with the obliging silence of the neighboring authorities—we invited over all the distinguished tenants of the cul-de-sac, and we had a collection of embassy attachés, in blue suits with golden buttons, young members of the Council of State,* budding public auditors, of which a brood of already serious, but still likeable, men was developing in this block of houses, in sight of the Tuileries and the neighboring ministries. They were only welcome provided they brought society women, protected, if they wished, by dominos and masks.

The landlords and concierges alone were condemned to troubled sleep—disturbed by the chords of a deliberately chosen dance hall orchestra, and the frantic leaps of a monstrous gallop, which from the main room to the stairs and from the stairs to the cul-de-sac had by necessity ended up in a little square surrounded by trees—where a cabaret was sheltered under the imposing ruins of the Doyenné chapel.

---

* One of them was named Van Daël, a young, charming man, but whose name brought misfortune to our castle.[27]

In the moonlight, one could still admire the remains of the enormous Italian dome which had crumbled, in the eighteenth century, on the six unfortunate canons—an accident of which the cardinal Dubois was momentarily suspected.[28]

But you will ask me to explain again, in feeble prose, those six lines of your play titled *Twenty Years*:

Your academic tone, Gérard! may I surmise
Is that the Opéra Comique's beautiful eyes
May light up somewhere else? That for two winters last
The queen of the Sabbath, *struggling in your grasp,*
Would, like a chimera, escape from you and hide?
"How bitter is woman!" is all Gérard replied.

Why *of the Sabbath* . . . my dear friend?[29] And why now throw absinthe into this golden goblet, molded from a beautiful breast?

Do you no longer recall the verses of that *Song of Songs*, in which the new Ecclesiastes speaks to this same queen of the morning:

The pomegranate in the Italian sun
To my delighted eyes is still less a treasure
Than your lips when they part, O madness, lovely one,
From which I drink the wine of sensual pleasure.

The Queen of Sheba, I was indeed preoccupied with her in those days—and doubly so.—The dazzling ghost of the daughter of the Himyarites tormented my nights under the high columns of that great sculpted bed, purchased in Touraine, and which was not yet covered in its red, leafy-patterned brocatelle. The salamanders of Francis I poured their flames on me from the top of the cornices, where some foolish loves were at play. SHE appeared to me as radiant as the day Solomon admired her when she came to him in the crimson splendors of the morning. She came to present me with the eternal riddle the Wise Man was unable to solve, and her eyes, sparkling more with malice than love, alone tempered the majesty of her oriental visage.—How beautiful she was! Not more beautiful, however, than another queen of the morning whose image tormented my days.

The latter was the living realization of my ideal and divine dream. She had, like the immortal Balkis, the gift passed on by the miraculous hoopoe. Birds fell silent when hearing her songs—and would certainly have followed her through those tunes.

It was a question of arranging for her debut at the Opera. Meyerbeer's triumph had become the guarantee of a new success. I dared to undertake the poem. In this way I would reunite in a stroke of fire the two halves of my double love.—That is why, my friend, you saw me so preoccupied on one of those splendid nights when our Louvre was so festive.—A word from Dumas had informed me that Meyerbeer would be waiting for us at seven o'clock the next morning.

ALEX· DVMAS·

IV

A WOMAN IN TEARS

That is all I was thinking of in the middle of the dance. A woman, whom you no doubt recall, was weeping warm tears in a corner of the room and, like me, was unable to bring herself to dance. This weeping beauty could not manage to hide her sorrow. Suddenly, she took my arm and said: "Take me home, I can't stay here."

I left with her on my arm. There were no carriages on the square. I advised her to calm herself and dry her eyes and then go back into the dance; she agreed only to go for a stroll along the little square. I knew of a certain wooden door that gave onto the riding school, and we spoke at length in the moonlight, under the lime trees. She told me at length all her despair.

The one who had brought her had grown enamored of another; hence a private quarrel; then she had threatened to go home, be it alone or accompanied; he had replied that she could do as she pleased. Hence the sighs, hence the tears.

The day was not far from breaking. The great saraband was beginning. Three or four history painters, hardly dancers by nature, had opened the little cabaret and were singing at the top of their voices: *He was a surly man*, or else: *He was a slanderer coming back from Flanders*, a memory of the joyous gatherings at Mother Saguet's.[30]—Our refuge was soon disturbed by some maskers who had found the little door open. They were talking of having breakfast in Madrid, the Madrid of the Bois de Boulogne—which was sometimes done. Soon the signal was given, we were pulled along, and we left on foot, escorted by three French guards, two of whom were simply MM. d'Egmont and de Beauvoir;—the third was Giraud, the painter in ordinary to the French Guards.[31]

The sentries of the Tuileries were baffled by this unexpected apparition, which seemed like the ghost of a scene from a hundred years ago, when French Guards would have led a troupe of rowdy maskers by violin. What's more, one of the two lovely little tobacco sellers, who had made the decorations for our dances, wouldn't let herself be taken off to Madrid without informing her husband, who had stayed at home. We accompanied her through the streets. She knocked at her door. Her husband appeared at a mezzanine window. She cried out to him: "I'm going to have something to eat with these gentlemen." He replied: "Go to the devil! What's the point of waking me up to tell me that!"

The distressed beauty offered little resistance to letting herself be taken away to Madrid; and as for me, I said my farewells to Rogier, explaining to him that I wanted to go work on my *scenario*.

"What? You're not coming with us? This lady has no other escort than you . . . and she chose you to take her home."

"But I'm meeting with Meyerbeer at seven, don't you understand?"

Rogier burst into wild laughter. One of his arms belonged to the Cydalise; he offered the other to the beautiful lady, who took her leave of me in a slightly mocking manner. I had at least managed to make her tears give way to a smile.

I had left the prey for the shadow . . . as always!

V

PRIMAVERA

In those days, I ronsardicized—to use one of Malherbe's phrases. Back then it was a matter for us young folk of emphasizing the old French versification, weakened by the languorous eighteenth century, troubled by the brutalities of overly fervent innovators; but we also needed to uphold the previous right of national literature in what relates to invention and general forms.

"But," you will tell me, "it is time to show these early verses, these *juvenilia*. 'Sound out those sonnets,' as Du Bellay would say."

Well, having acknowledged the painstaking study of those old poets, believe me when I say that I had not the slightest intention of making a pastiche of them, but rather that their forms of style impressed me despite myself, as happens to many poets of our time.

The *odelettes*, or Ronsard's little odes, served me as a model. It was still a classical form, in which he himself imitated Anacreon, Bion,[32] and up to a certain point, Horace. The concentrated form of the odelette seemed as valuable to preserve as the sonnet, in which Ronsard was so happily inspired by Petrarch, just as, in his elegies, he followed in the footsteps of Ovid; Ronsard was, however, generally more Greek than Latin: that is what distinguishes his school from Malherbe's.

You will see, my friend, whether these already aging poems have still retained some fragrance.—I wrote them in every rhythm, more or less in imitation, as one does when one first begins.

The ode on the butterflies is again in the style of Ronsard and can be sung to the tune of Joseph's hymn. Note one thing: odelettes were sung and even became popular, as this sentence from the *Comic Novel*[33] testifies: "We heard the servant who, with a mouth soaked in garlic, was singing old Ronsard's ode:

Let us go with our voices
And with our ivory lutes
To delight the spirits!

Moreover, this was only revived from ancient odes, which were also sung. I wrote the first ones without thinking of that, so they are not in the least lyrical. The last one: "Where are our lovers?" came to me, despite myself, in the form of a song; I had found the verses at the same time as the melody, which I was obliged to notate, and which matched the words very well.

ODELETTES

To Arsène Houssaye

AVRIL

Déjà les beaux jours, la poussière,
Un ciel d'azur et de lumière,
Les murs enflammés, les longs soirs;
Et rien de vert: à peine encore
Un reflet rougeâtre décore
Les grands arbres aux rameaux noirs!

Ce beaux temps me pèse et m'ennuie.
Ce n'est qu'après des jours de pluie
Que doit surgir, en un tableau,
Le printemps verdissant et rose,
Comme une nymphe fraîche éclose,
Qui, souriante, sort de l'eau.

APRIL

And now the dust and the fine days,
An azure sky and walls ablaze
With burning light, long nights, no breeze,
And nothing green; a ruddy shine
Just barely stains, like a red wine,
The black branches of the large trees.

Upon me this fine weather weighs.
Only after long rainy days
Should spring then come, Nature's daughter,
Turning rosy and turning green,
Like a blooming nymph in a scene
Who, smiling, springs from the water.

FANTAISIE

Il est un air pour qui je donnerais
Tout Rossini, tout Mozart et tout Weber
Un air très-vieux, languissant et funèbre,
Qui pour moi seul a des charmes secrets!

Or chaque fois que je viens à l'entendre,
De deux cents ans mon âme rajeunit . . .
C'est sous Louis treize; et je crois voir s'étendre
Un coteau vert, que le couchant jaunit,

Puis un château de brique à coins de pierre,
Aux vitraux teints de rougeâtres couleurs,
Ceint de grands parcs, avec une rivière
Baignant ses pieds, qui coule entre les fleurs;

Puis une dame, à sa haute fenêtre,
Blonde aux yeux noirs, en ses habits anciens,
Que, dans une autre existence peut-être,
J'ai déjà vue . . . et dont je me souviens!

FANTASIA

I would give for that tune and its motif
All Mozart, all Weber, and all Rossini,
A very old tune of sorrow and grief,
Which has secret charms known only to me!

Now every time that it reaches my ears,
My soul grows younger by two hundred years.
It is under Louis Treize . . . and I see
The sun set on a green hill before me,

Then a brick castle with corners of stone,
With stained-glass windows that give off red glows,
Encircled by parks; at its base, alone,
A stirring river through the flowers flows.

Then a lady, with blonde hair and black eyes
In ancient clothing, at a high window,
Whom I've seen before, under other skies,
In another life . . . and already know!

LA GRAND'MERE

Voici trois ans qu'est morte ma grand'mère,
—La bonne femme!—et, quand on l'enterra,
Parents, amis, tout le monde pleura
D'une douleur bien vraie et bien amère.

Moi seul j'errais dans la maison, surpris
Plus que chagrin; et, comme j'étais proche
De son cercueil,—quelqu'un me fit reproche
De voir cela sans larmes et sans cris.

Douleur bruyante est bien vite passée:
Depuis trois ans, d'autres émotions,
Des biens, des maux,—des révolutions,—
Ont dans les cœurs sa mémoire effacée.

Moi seul j'y songe, et la pleure souvent;
Depuis trois ans, par le temps prenant force
Ainsi qu'un nom gravé dans une écorce,
Son souvenir se creuse plus avant!

GRANDMOTHER

It is three years now since grandmother died,
—The good woman!—and when she was buried
It was real grief, when off she was carried
That parents and friends had felt when they cried.

I alone wandered through the house, surprised
Rather than upset; and when I approached
Her coffin, quiet—I was then reproached
For shedding no tears and giving no cries.

Clamorous grief and sorrow soon depart:
For the last three years, other emotions,
Both good and evil—and revolutions—
Her memory have erased from each heart.

I alone think of her and often weep;
For three years, time has worked her memory,
Like a name carved in the bark of a tree,
Burrowing it in ever so deep!

LA COUSINE

L'hiver a ses plaisirs; et souvent, le dimanche,
Quand un peu de soleil jaunit la terre blanche,
Avec une cousine on sort se promener . . .
—Et ne vous faites pas attendre pour dîner.

Dit la mère. Et quand on a bien, aux Tuileries,
Va sous les arbres noirs les toilettes fleuries,
La jeune fille a froid . . . et vous fait observer
Que le brouillard du soir commence à se lever.

Et l'on revient, parlant du beau jour qu'on regrette,
Qui s'est passé si vite . . . et de flamme discrète:
Et l'on sent en rentrant, avec grand appétit,
Du bas de l'escalier,—le dindon qui rôtit.

COUSIN

Winter has its pleasures; and often, on Sundays,
When the sun lays on the white earth a yellow glaze,
With a cousin you go outside to take a stroll . . .
—And don't stay out too long and let supper get cold,

Says mother. And when you have, at the Tuileries,
Seen the flowered outfits under all the black trees,
The young girl then feels cold . . . and observes as she sighs
That the early evening mist is starting to rise.

And you head back, talking of that beautiful day
Now past and missed . . . and of a flame hidden away:
And you smell, coming home, with a great appetite,
The turkey that's roasting as the day fades to night.

PENSÉE DE BYRON

Par mon amour et ma constance,
J'avais cru fléchir ta rigueur,
Et le souffle de l'espérance
Avait pénétré dans mon cœur;
Mais le temps, qu'en vain je prolonge,
M'a découvert la vérité,
L'espérance a fui comme un songe,
Et mon amour seul m'est resté!

Il est resté comme un abîme
Entre ma vie et le bonheur,
Comme un mal dont je suis victime,
Comme un poids jeté sur mon cœur!
Dans le chagrin qui me dévore,
Je vois mes beaux jours s'envoler;
Si mon œil étincelle encore,
C'est qu'une larme en va couler!

BYRON'S THOUGHT

Through my love and my constancy,
Your severity I assailed,
And the breath of hope entered me
And over my heart had prevailed;
But time has shown the truth to me,
Time, which I have prolonged in vain,
And like a dream hope had to flee,
And only my love now remains!

It remains there like an abyss
A pain that's meant to keep apart
My life from any happiness
Like a weight cast onto my heart!
In the grief that turns me to ash,
I see my fine days fade and go;
If my eye still gives off a flash,
It's just a tear about to flow!

GAIETÉ

Petit *piqueton* de Mareuil,
Plus clairet qu'un vin d'Argenteuil,
Que ta saveur est souveraine!
Les Romains ne t'ont pas compris
Lorsqu'habitant l'ancien Paris
Ils te préféraient la Surène.

Ta liqueur rose, ô joli vin!
Semble faite du sang divin
De quelque nymphe bocagère;
Tu perles au borde désiré
D'un verre à côtes, coloré
Par les teintes de la fougère.

Tu me guéris pendant l'été
De la soif qu'un vin plus vanté
M'avait laissé depuis la veille;
Ton goût suret, mais doux aussi,
Happant mon palais épaissi,
Me rafraîchit quand je m'éveille.

Eh quoi! si gai dès le matin,
Je foule d'un pied incertain
Le sentier où verdit ton pampre! . . .

GAIETY

Little *piqueton* of Mareuil,[34]
Thinner than wine of Argenteuil,
How sovereign is your flavor!
The Romans who understood you
When in ancient Paris were few:
The Suresnes they used to favor.

Your rosy liqueur, lovely wine!
Seems to be made from the divine
Blood of some nymph for whom I yearn;
You bead at the desired rim
Of a ribbed glass, as if by whim,
Colored by the hues of the fern.

In the summer you quench the thirst
A lauded wine I had drunk first
Had left me with the day before;
Your sour taste, though also sweet,
Which my palate will always greet
When I wake up, refreshes more.

Well! Cheery on rising from bed,
I walk with an uncertain tread
The path laced with your green pampre! . . .

—Et je n'ai pas de Richelet
pour finir ce docte couplet . . .
Et trouver une rime en *ampre*.*

* Lisez le *Dictionnaire des Rimes* à l'article Ampre vous n'y trouverez que *pampre*; pourquoi ce mot si sonore n'a-t-il pas de rime?

—And I'm lacking a *Richelet*[35]
To help conclude this learnèd lay . . .
And end with a rhyme for *ampre.**

* Read the *Dictionary of Rhymes*. Under the article Ampre, you will only find *pampre*; why does such a sonorous word have no rhyme?

POLITIQUE

1832

Dans Sainte-Pélagie,
Sous ce règne élargie,
Où, rêveur et pensif,
            Je vis captif,

Pas une herbe ne pousse
Et pas un brin de mousse
Le long des murs grillés
            Et frais taillés!

Oiseau qui fends l'espace . . .
Et toi, brise, qui passe
Sur l'étroit horizon
            De la prison,

Dans votre vol superbe,
Apportez-moi quelque herbe,
Quelque gramen, mouvant
            Sa tête au vent!

Qu'à mes pieds tourbillonne
Une feuille d'automne
Peinte de cent couleurs
            Comme les fleurs!

POLITICS

1832

Here in Saint Pélagie,
Under this reign that's free,
Where, dreaming and pensive,
    I'm a captive,

Not a blade of grass grows,
No moss and no meadows
To be seen from this wall,
    Barred and built tall!

Bird cleaving space on high . . .
And you, breeze, passing by
Along the horizon
    Of this prison,

Bring me from your fine flight
Something green, something bright,
Some blade of grass moving
    Softly, soothing.

May an autumn leaf swirl
At my feet and unfurl
A hundred bright colors
    Like the flowers!

Pour que mon âme triste
Sache encor qu'il existe
Une nature, un Dieu
            Dehors ce lieu,

Faites-moi cette joie,
Qu'un instant je revoie
Quelque chose de vert
            Avant l'hiver!

So my soul can persist
In knowing there exists
Nature, some divine grace
        Beyond this place

Relieve my sorrowed pain
And show me green again
Before everything numbs
        And winter comes.

LES PAPILLONS

I

Le papillon, fleur sans tige,
Qui voltige,
Que l'on cueille en un réseau:
Dans la nature infinie,
Harmonie
Entre la plante et l'oiseau!

Quand revient l'été superbe,
Je m'en vais au bois tout seul:
Je m'étends dans la grande herbe,
Perdu dans ce vert linceul.
Sur ma tête renversée,
Là, chacun d'eux à son tour,
Passe comme une pensée
De poésie ou d'amour!

Voici le papillon *Faune*,
Noir et jaune;
Voici le *Mars* azuré,
Agitant des étincelles
Sur ses ailes
D'un velours riche et moiré.

BUTTERFLIES

I

Stemless flower, butterfly,
          Flutters by
And by a net is gathered;
In nature to guarantee
          Harmony
Between the plant and the bird!

When spring to summer passes,
I go to the woods alone
Lying in the tall grasses,
To be in a green shroud sewn.
There, with my head tilted back,
Each one passing over me,
Like a thought I cannot track
Of love or of poetry!

The *Tree Grayling* flutters back:
          Yellow, black;
Here's the *Purple Emperor*,
Of glinting velvet, it flings
          From its wings
Azure sparks and blue embers.

Voici le *Vulcain* rapide,
Qui vole comme un oiseau:
Son aile noire et splendide
Porte un grand ruban ponceau.

Dieux! le *Soufré*, dans l'espace,
Comme un éclair a relui . . .
Mai le joyeux *Nacré* passe,
Et je ne vois plus que lui!

Here's the swift *Red Admiral*,
Like a bird it is in flight:
Its wing, black and masterful,
Bears a ribbon, large and bright.

Pale Clouded Yellow flies by,
A lightning flash flying free . . .
But now filling my whole sky:
Queen of Spain fritillary!

II

Comme un éventail de soie,
Il déploie
Son manteau semé d'argent;
Et sa robe bigarrée
Est dorée
D'un or verdâtre et changeant.

Voici le *Machaon-Zèbre*,
De fauve et de noir rayé;
Le *Deuil*, en habit funèbre,
Et le *Miroir* bleu strié;
Voici l'*Argus*, feuille-morte,
Le *Morio*, le *Grand-Bleu*,
Et le *Paon-de-Jour* qui porte
Sur chaque aile un œil de feu!

Mais le soir brunit nos plaines;
Les *Phalènes*
Prennent leur essor bruyant,
Et les *Sphinx* aux couleurs sombres,
Dans les ombres
Voltigent en tournoyant.

II

Like a silken, silver fan,
            Her wingspan
Spreads open a spangled coat;
And her many-colored dress
            Is caressed
By a gold with greenish notes.

Here's the *Zebra Swallowtail*,
Striped black and brown through and through;
Marbled White, in mourning veil,
Large Checkered Skipper, streaked blue;
Here's *Brown Argus* in its frock,
The *Large Blue*, the *Mourning Cloak*,
The *European Peacock*,
Winged eyes blazing with each stroke!

But evening spreads like a cloth
            And the moths
Rise noisily with the night,
And the dark *Hawk moths*, all made
            From the shade
Circle about in their flight.

C'est le *Grand-Paon* à l'œil rose
Dessiné sur un fond gris,
Qui ne vole qu'à nuit close,
Comme les chauves-souris;
Le *Bombice* du troène,
Rayé de jaune et de vert,
Et le *Papillon du chêne*
Qui ne meurt pas en hiver!

The *Great Peacock*'s rosy eye
Drawn upon a gray background,
Watches only the dark sky,
Like the bats that fly by sound;
Calling the privet its home
The *Silkmoth*, yellow and green;
The *Oak Eggar*, in the gloam,
In winter still on the scene!

III

Malheur, papillons que j'aime,
　　　　Doux emblème,
A vous pour votre beauté! . . .
Un doigt, de votre corsage,
　　　　Au passage,
Froisse, hélas! le velouté! . . .

Une toute jeune fille
Au cœur tendre, au doux souris,
Perçant vos cœurs d'une aiguille,
Vous contemple, l'œil surpris:
Et vos pattes sont coupées
Par l'ongle blanc qui les mord,
Et vos antennes crispées
Dans les douleurs de la mort! . . .

III

Misfortune, my butterflies,
            symbolize;
To the beauty you possess! . . .
A finger crumples and pokes
            As it strokes,
The smooth velvet of your dress! . . .

A young girl with a sweet smile,
With loving heart and bright eyes,
Puts a pin through your heart while
Gazing at you with surprise:
And off your legs are then cut
By a sharp white fingernail,
Your antennas writhe and jut:
In the throes of death you flail! . . .

LE POINT NOIR

Quiconque a regardé le soleil fixement
Croit voir devant ses yeux voler obstinément
Autour de lui, dans l'air, une tache livide.

Ainsi, tout jeune encore et plus audacieux,
Sur la gloire un instant j'osai fixer les yeux:
Un point noir est resté dans mon regard avide

Depuis, mêlée à tout comme un signe de deuil,
Partout, sur quelque endroit que s'arrête mon œil,
Je la vois se poser aussi, la tache noire!

Quoi, toujours? Entre moi sans cesse et le bonheur!
Oh! c'est que l'aigle seul—malheur à nous, malheur!—
Contemple impunément le Soleil et la Gloire.

THE BLACK SPOT

He who has ever gazed at the sun fixedly
Thinks he sees fly before his eyes persistently
About him, in the air, a spot, dark and livid.

And so, in this manner, when I was young and bold,
Bright glory I had once dared let my eyes behold:
My eager gaze retained a spot, black and vivid.

Since then, like a sign of mourning covering all,
Everywhere that my eye should now happen to fall,
The black spot also sets and is all I can see.

What, still? Always between myself and happiness!
Oh, the eagle alone can gaze—woe betide us!
On the Sun and Glory with full impunity.[36]

NI BONJOUR NI BONSOIR

SUR UN AIR GREC

Νή χαλιμέρα, νή ωρα χαλί.

Le matin n'est plus! le soir pas encore!
Pourtant de nos yeux l'éclair a pâli.

Νή χαλιμέρα, νή ωρα χαλί.

Mais le soir vermeil ressemble à l'aurore,
Et la nuit plus tard amène l'oubli!

NEITHER GOOD DAY NOR GOOD NIGHT

ON A GREEK TUNE

Νή χαλιμέρα, νή ωρα χαλί.

Evening's not yet here! But morning is gone.
And the fire has faded from our sight.

Νή χαλιμερα, νή ωρα χαλί.

But rosy evening resembles the dawn,
And later the void will come with the night![37]

LES CYDALISES

Où sont nos amoureuses?
Elles sont au tombeau:
Elles sont plus heureuses,
Dans un séjour plus beau!

Elles sont près des anges,
Dans le fond du ciel bleu,
Et chantent les louanges
De la mère de Dieu!

O blanche fiancée!
O jeune vierge en fleur!
Amante délaissée,
Que flétrit la douleur!

L'éternité profonde
Souriait dans vos yeux . . .
Flambeaux éteints du monde
Rallumez-vous aux cieux!

THE CYDALISES

Where might our lovers be?
They are there in the grave:
Far happier and free
In a lovelier place!

With the angels above,
And by the deep sky awed,
Singing praises with love
To the Mother of God!

Fiancée, awaken!
O virgin in flower!
Mistress forsaken,
Withered by sorrow!

Eternity unfurled
Smiled deep in your eyes . . .
Dead torches of the world
Illuminate the skies!

SECOND CASTLE

That one was a castle in Spain, built with frames, *set pieces*, and platforms . . . Shall I tell you its glorious story, at once poetic and lyrical? Let us first go back to the meeting Dumas arranged for me, which had made me miss another.

I had written, with all the fire of youth, a very complicated scenario that seemed to be to Meyerbeer's liking. I took the hope he gave me to heart; except that Dumas already had another opera for him, *The Corsican Brothers*, and the prospects for my own were somewhat distant. I had already written an act when I suddenly learned that the agreement between the great poet and the great composer had been broken, I don't know why.—Dumas was leaving for his trip to the Mediterranean, Meyerbeer had already continued on his way to Germany. The poor *Queen of Sheba*, abandoned by everyone, later became a simple oriental tale which played a part in the *Nights of Ramadan*.

And so poetry fell into prose and my theatrical castle into the *third* below-stage.—However, theatrical and lyrical ideas had awakened in me, I wrote a one-act light opera in prose, leaving open the possibility of interpolating other pieces into it later. I have just found the original manuscript, which never tempted any of the musicians to whom I presented it. It is thus no more than a simple proverb, and I speak of it here only by way of an episode in these brief literary memories.[38]

CORILLA

FABIO
MARCELLI
MAZETTO, theater assistant
CORILLA, prima donna

Saint Lucia Boulevard, in Naples, near the Opera.

FABIO, MAZETTO

FABIO: If you're tricking me, Mazetto, you're playing a miserable game . . .

MAZETTO: There's no better game; but I am serving you faithfully. I'm telling you, she will come this evening; she received your letters and your bouquets.

FABIO: And the golden chain, and the clasp of semiprecious stones?

MAZETTO: Fear not: they reached her as well, and perhaps you will recognize them on her neck and waist; it is only because the style of those jewels is so modern that she has not yet found a role in which she could wear them as part of her costume.

FABIO: But has she at least seen me? Has she noticed the spot where I sit every evening to admire her and applaud, and can I believe that my gifts will not be the sole cause of her conduct?

MAZETTO: Bah! Sir, what you gave is nothing to someone of her high standing; once you get to know each other better, she will repay you with some portrait framed in pearls worth twice as much. Same for the ten ducats you have already given me, and the twenty others you promised as soon as your first rendezvous was guaranteed; it is only a loan, as I told you, and you will one day get them back with substantial interest.

FABIO: Enough, I expect no such thing.

MAZETTO: No, sir, you must know what kind of people you are dealing with, and that far from ruining you, you are here on the true road to your fortune; so please pay me the agreed-on sum, for I must go to the theater to carry out my nightly duties.

FABIO: But why has she not answered me, not written down a meeting place?

MAZETTO: Because she's only seen you from a distance, or more specifically, from the stage to the boxes—just as you yourself have only seen her from the boxes to the stage. Do you understand? She wants to know your manners and your ways first, the sound of your voice, whatever. Would you want the foremost singer of San Carlo to welcome just anyone without first obtaining further information?

FABIO: But dare I approach her? And is your word enough for me to risk being rejected, or appearing in her eyes like some common ladies' man?

MAZETTO: I repeat, all you have to do is walk along this quay, which is almost deserted at this hour; she will pass by, hiding her lowered face under the fringe of her mantilla; she will address you and name a meeting place for this evening, for this spot is not very appropriate for a lengthy conversation. Will that be satisfactory?

FABIO: O Mazetto! If you're telling the truth, you're saving my life!

MAZETTO: Hence the twenty louis we agreed on.

FABIO: You'll receive them when I have spoken to her.

MAZETTO: You're distrustful; but your love interests me, and I would have been of service through pure friendship, if I didn't have to feed my family. Stay where you are, then, as though dreaming and composing some sonnet; I'm going to have a look around the area to prevent any surprises.

He leaves.

FABIO, *alone.*

I am to see her! See her for the first time in the light of day, hear, for the first time, words that she herself has thought! A word from her will either realize my dream, or make it vanish forever! Ah, I fear risking here more than I can win; my passion was great and pure, and grazed the world without touching it; it lived only in glorious palaces and along enchanted shores; here it is brought down to earth and forced to make its way like any other. Like Pygmalion, I worshiped the exterior form of a woman; except that the statue moved every evening before my eyes with a divine grace, and from her mouth fell pearls of melody. And now here she is descending to me. But the love that made this miracle is a disgraceful comic-opera valet, and the ray which makes this adored idol live for me is one of those that Jupiter poured onto the breast of Danaë![39]. . . She's coming, it is indeed her; oh, my courage is failing me, and I would be tempted to flee if she had not already seen me!

FABIO, A LADY *in a mantilla.*

THE LADY, *passing near him*: Seigneur cavalier, give me your arm, please, so that no one notices us, and let us walk naturally. You wrote me . . .

FABIO: And I received no response . . .

THE LADY: Do you value my writing more than my words?

FABIO: Your mouth or your hand would hold it against me if I dared choose.

THE LADY: May one be the guarantee of the other; your letters touched me, and I agree to the meeting you ask of me. You know why I cannot receive you at home?

FABIO: I was told.

THE LADY: I am surrounded and very constrained in whatever I do. Wait for me this evening, at five o'clock, at the Villa Reale; I will come there in disguise, and we can have a few moments of conversation.

FABIO: I will be there.

THE LADY: Now, let go my arm, and don't follow me, I'm going to the theater. Do not appear in the auditorium this evening . . . Be discreet and trusting. *(She leaves.)*

FABIO, *alone*: It was indeed her! . . . As she left, she revealed all in a movement, like Virgil's Venus. I barely recognized her face and yet the flash of her eyes pierced my heart, just as at the theater, when her gaze crosses mine in the crowd. Her voice loses none of its charm when uttering simple words; and yet up until now I thought she could only sing, like the birds! But what she told me is worth all the verses of Metastasio,[40] and that pure timbre, that sweet accent, borrow none of their seduction from the melodies of Paisiello or Cimarosa.[41] Ah, all those heroines I worship in her—Sophonisba, Alcina, Herminie, and even that blond Molinara, whom she plays beautifully in less magnificent clothes—I see them all at once enclosed under that charming mantilla, under that satin headdress . . . Mazetto again!

FABIO, MAZETTO

MAZETTO: Well, Seigneur, am I a treacherous rogue, a man not of his word, a man without honor?

FABIO: You are the most virtuous of mortals! But here, take this purse and leave me alone.

MAZETTO: You seem bothered.

FABIO: Happiness makes me sad; it makes me think of the unhappiness that always follows right behind.

MAZETTO: Do you need your money to play lansquenet tonight? I can give it back and even lend you some more.

FABIO: That isn't necessary. Farewell.

MAZETTO: Beware the *jettatura*, Seigneur Fabio! *(He leaves.)*

FABIO, *alone.*

I'm tired of seeing that rascal's head cast its shadow over my love; but thank God, that messenger soon won't be needed. What has he done, anyway, but deftly deliver my notes and my flowers, which had for so long been rejected? Come, come, the matter was skillfully conducted and approaches its denouement . . . But then why am I so morose this evening, when I should be overjoyed and strike these flagstones with a triumphant foot? Did she not give in a bit quickly—especially since receiving my presents? . . . All right, I look too much on the dark side of things, and I should instead start preparing my amorous rhetoric. It's clear we won't be just chatting amorously under the trees, and that I will manage to take her to Chiaia to dine in some inn; but I will have to be dazzling, passionate, and madly in love—to raise my conversation to the tone of my style and realize the ideal which my letters and verses have presented to her . . . and yet I feel no warmth, no energy . . . I need to rouse my imagination with some glasses of Spanish wine.

FABIO, MARCELLI

MARCELLI: That's a sad way of going about it, Seigneur Fabio; wine is the most traitorous of companions; it takes you into a palace and leaves you in a gutter.

FABIO: Ah, Seigneur Marcelli! You were listening to me?

MARCELLI: No, but I heard you.

FABIO: Did I say anything to displease you?

MARCELLI: On the contrary: you were claiming to be sad and wishing for wine, that is all I caught of your monologue. I myself am in very high spirits. I walk along this quay like a bird; I am thinking mad thoughts, I cannot stay in place, and I fear I shall wear myself out. Let's keep each other company for a bit; if it's intoxication you need, I am as good as any bottle, and yet I am filled with nothing but joy; I need to open my heart like a flask of Sillery, and I wish to share with you a stunning secret.

FABIO: For pity's sake, choose a confidant less absorbed in his own affairs. My head is elsewhere, my dear fellow; I am good for nothing this evening and were you to confide to me that King Midas had the ears of an ass, I swear that I would be unable to repeat it tomorrow.

MARCELLI: Good God, that's what I need! A confidant as silent as the tomb.

FABIO: All right, I know your ways . . . You wish to announce your good fortune, and you have chosen me to be the herald of your glory.

MARCELLI: On the contrary, I want to prevent an indiscretion by voluntarily confiding certain things which you are sure to have suspected.

FABIO: I don't know what you mean.

MARCELLI: One does not keep a known secret, whereas one is bound to do so when it has been given in confidence.

FABIO: But I have no idea of what might concern you.

MARCELLI: Then I shall have to tell you everything.

FABIO: You are not going to the theater, then?

MARCELLI: No, not this evening; and you?

FABIO: I have a matter to think over and need to walk alone.

MARCELLI: I'll wager you're composing an opera?

FABIO: You've guessed it.

MARCELLI: And who wouldn't? You haven't missed a single performance at the San Carlo; you arrive right at the overture, which nobody does; you don't leave during the last act, and you remain alone in the theater with the groundlings. It's clear you're studying your art with care and perseverance. But there is one thing I'm not clear on: are you a poet or a musician?

FABIO: Both.

MARCELLI: Well, I'm just an amateur and have only composed lighthearted songs. So you know very well that my regular appearance in that theater, where we have been constantly running into each other for several weeks now, can only be due to an amorous affair . . .

FABIO: Of which I have no desire to be informed.

MARCELLI: Oh, you won't maneuver your way out of this, and it is only when you know all that I shall feel certain of the mystery my love calls for.

FABIO: It is a question of some actress, then . . . Borsella?

MARCELLI: No, the new Spanish singer, the divine Corilla! . . . By Bacchus! You must have noticed us winking furiously at each other?

FABIO, *testily*: Never!

MARCELLI: The signs we make at certain moments when the audience's attention is directed elsewhere?

FABIO: I have seen no such a thing.

MARCELLI: What! You've been that absorbed? I was wrong, then, to believe you knew part of my secret; but as I'm already confiding . . .

FABIO, *brusquely*: Yes, indeed! I'm now curious to know where this is going.

MARCELLI: Perhaps you never paid much attention to Signora Corilla. I suppose you're more preoccupied with her voice than her face? Well, do give it a look, it is charming!

FABIO: I agree.

MARCELLI: An Italian or Spanish blonde always makes for a very remarkable type of beauty, and one all the more impressive through its rarity.

FABIO: That's my opinion as well.

MARCELLI: Don't you think she resembles Caravaggio's Judith in the Musée Royal?[42]

FABIO: Sir, enough! In short, you're her lover, right?

MARCELLI: Excuse me; at this point I'm only her sweetheart.

FABIO: You surprise me.

MARCELLI: I must tell you that she is quite forbidding.

FABIO: So they claim.

MARCELLI: She's a tigress, a Bradamante . . .[43]

FABIO: An Alcimadure.[44]

MARCELLI: As her door remained closed to my bouquets, and her window to my serenades, I concluded that she had reasons for being unresponsive . . . at home, but that her virtue must be less steady on the boards of an opera-house stage . . . I tested the ground, I learned that a certain scamp named Mazetto had access to her, because of his service to the theater . . .

FABIO: You entrusted your flowers and your letters to that rascal.

MARCELLI: So you knew this?

FABIO: Along with some presents he advised you to give.

MARCELLI: Did I not say that you were informed?

FABIO: You received no letters from her?

MARCELLI: Not one.

FABIO: It would really be remarkable if the lady herself, passing by you in the street, had, in a low voice, named a meeting place . . .

MARCELLI: You are the devil, or I am myself!

FABIO: For tomorrow?

MARCELLI: No, for today.

FABIO: At five o'clock this evening?

MARCELLI: At five o'clock.

FABIO: So, at the Villa Reale?

MARCELLI: No, in front of the Fountain of Neptune.

FABIO: I don't understand any of this.

MARCELLI: Good lord, you want to guess everything, know everything better than I do. It's odd. Now that I've told you everything, your honor calls for discretion.

FABIO: Very well. Listen to me, my friend . . . one of us has been duped.

MARCELLI: What are you saying?

FABIO: Or both of us, if you like. We have appointments with the same person, at the same hour: you, before the Fountain of Neptune; me, at the Villa Reale!

MARCELLI: I have no time to be astonished; but what is the reason for this heavy-handed joke?

FABIO: If it is reason you lack, it is not my job to give it to you; if it is a stroke of a sword you need, draw your own.

MARCELLI: I'm thinking: you have an advantage over me right now.

FABIO: You admit it?

MARCELLI: Of course! You're an unhappy lover, that much is clear; you were going to throw yourself over this handrail or hang yourself from the branches of those lime trees if I hadn't run into you. I, on the other hand, am successful, favored, nearly victorious; I'm dining this evening with the object of my desire. I would be doing you a service if I killed you; but were I to be killed, you must agree that it would be unfortunate if it was before, and not after. Things are not equal; let us postpone the matter until tomorrow.

FABIO: I was thinking the exact same thing and could repeat your own words back to you. So, I agree to not punish you for your mad bragging until tomorrow. I only thought you to be indiscreet.

MARCELLI: Very well! Let us part without another word. I have no wish to force you into humiliating confessions, nor to further compromise a lady who has nothing but good will toward me. I am counting on your discretion and will provide you with news of my evening tomorrow morning.

FABIO: I promise you the same; but after that we will most certainly cross swords. Until tomorrow, then.

MARCELLI: Until tomorrow, Seigneur Fabio.

FABIO, *alone.*

Some sort of anxiety has led me to follow him at a distance instead of going my own way. Let's turn back! *(He takes a few steps.)* Such self-assurance is just too much—but he could hardly go back on his claim and confess that he lied. That's how our fashionable young madmen are; nothing stands in their way, they are the conquerors and favorites of all women, and Don Juan's list would cost them no more effort than the trouble of writing it. Besides, if this beauty was deceiving one of us with the other, it would not have been at the same hour. Let us go, I believe the moment approaches, and I would do well to head for the Villa Reale, which must already be clear of its strollers and given over to solitude. But, in fact, is that not Marcelli over there giving his arm to a woman? . . . I have truly gone mad; if it is him, it cannot be her . . . What to do? If I go to them, I miss my rendezvous . . . but if I do not clear my head of suspicion, I risk, by going over there, playing a fool's part. This uncertainty is indeed cruel. Time is pressing, I'm going back and forth, and my position is most peculiar. Why did I have to encounter that scatterbrain who is perhaps deceiving me? He must have known of my love through Mazetto, and everything he just told me stems from some obscure treachery I'll have to sort out.—That's it, I've made my decision, I'm running to the Villa Reale. *(He returns.)* Upon my soul, they're approaching; it is the same mantilla trimmed with long lace; it is the same dress of gray silk . . . they're almost here. Oh, if it is her, if I've been deceived . . . I won't wait for tomorrow to take revenge on them both! . . . What shall I do? A ridiculous imbroglio . . . let us withdraw behind this trellis to make sure that it's them.

FABIO, *hidden*; MARCELLI; *Signora* CORILLA *giving him her arm.*

MARCELLI: Yes, fair lady, you see how pompous some people can get. There is a gentleman in the city bragging of having also obtained a meeting from you for this evening. And if I was not sure of having you now on my arm, fulfilling a sweet promise too long deferred . . .

CORILLA: Come, you're joking, Seigneur Marcelli. And this conceited gentleman . . . you know him?

MARCELLI: It was to me that he confided . . .

FABIO, *showing himself*: You are mistaken, sir, it was you who confided in me . . . Madame, there is no point in taking this any further; I've decided not to endure such a coquettish game. Seigneur Marcelli can bring you back to your place, since you have given him your arm; but after, may he well remember that *I* am waiting for him.

MARCELLI: Listen, my dear fellow, isn't being a fool enough for you?

FABIO: Are you calling me a fool?

MARCELLI: I am. If you wish to cause a stir, wait for daybreak; I don't fight beneath streetlamps, and I have no interest in getting arrested by the night guard.

CORILLA: This man is mad; don't you see that? Let us withdraw.

FABIO: Ah, madame! Enough . . . don't completely shatter this beautiful image I bore, pure and holy, in the depths of my heart. Alas, I was content to love you at a distance, to write you . . . I had little hope, and I asked for less than you promised me!

CORILLA: You wrote? To me! . . .

MARCELLI: Hey, what does it matter? This is not the place for explanations . . .

CORILLA: And what did I promise you, sir? . . . I don't know you and I've never spoken to you.

MARCELLI: Good! The idea you would have indulged in idle talk with him, so what! Do you think that affects my love?

CORILLA: But what are you thinking, Seigneur? Since things have gotten to this point, I want an explanation right now. This gentleman believes he has a complaint against me: let him speak and more than anything, name himself, for I have no idea what he wants.

FABIO: Put your mind at ease, madame. I'm ashamed over my outburst and for having yielded to my initial surprise. You accuse me of imposture, and your beautiful mouth cannot lie. As you said: I am mad, I was dreaming. On this very spot, an hour ago, something like your ghost passed by, addressed some sweet words to me, and promised to return . . . There was some magic involved, no doubt, and yet all the details remain in my mind. I was there, I had just seen the sun set behind Posillipo, throwing the hem of its red cloak onto Ischia; the sea was darkening in the gulf, and the white sails were hastening to land like late doves . . . You see, I am a sad dreamer, my letters must have told you that, but you will hear no more of me, I swear, and I bid you farewell.

CORILLA: Your letters . . . you know, this all sounds like a theatrical imbroglio. Let me not keep you any longer; Seigneur Marcelli, please take my arm again and escort me back home with all possible speed. *(Fabio takes his leave and withdraws.)*

MARCELLI: To your home, madam?

CORILLA: Yes, I am quite upset! . . . This has all been most peculiar. If the palace square is not yet deserted, let us find a chair, or at least a lantern. In fact, here are the theater valets leaving; call one of them over . . .

MARCELLI: Hey! Anyone! Over here . . . But are you really not feeling well?

CORILLA: Enough to stop walking . . .

FABIO, MAZETTO, THE PRECEDING PERSONS

FABIO, *dragging Mazetto*: Well, well, heaven has brought him to us; here is the villain who deceived me.

MARCELLI: Mazetto! The greatest knave of the Two Sicilies. He was also your messenger?

MAZETTO: The devil take it! You're suffocating me.

FABIO: You are going to explain to us . . .

MAZETTO: And what are you doing here, seigneur? I thought you in good fortune?

FABIO: You would do better to look after your own. You are going to die if you do not confess your treachery.

MARCELLI: Wait a moment, Seigneur Fabio, I too have a score to settle with him. Together, now.

MAZETTO: Gentlemen, if you want me to understand, don't both hit at once. What is the matter?

FABIO: What do you think is the matter, wretch? What did you do with my letters?

MARCELLI: And in what way have you compromised the honor of Signora Corilla?

MAZETTO: Gentlemen, someone might hear us.

MARCELLI: There is no one here but the signora herself and the two of us, which is to say, two men who are going to kill each other tomorrow because of her or because of you.

MAZETTO: Allow me: as the case is serious, and my humanity forbids me from continuing this charade . . .

FABIO: Speak.

MAZETTO: At least put away your swords.

FABIO: Then we'll take up clubs.

MARCELLI: No; we must restrain ourselves if he tells the whole truth, but only at that price.

CORILLA: His insolence is outrageous.

MARCELLI: Should we knock him senseless before he has spoken?

CORILLA: No, I want to know everything; there cannot be the slightest doubt over my honesty in such a sinister affair.

MAZETTO: My confession is your panegyric, madam; all of Naples knows the austerity of your life. Now, Seigneur Marcelli, who stands before you, was passionately in love with you; he went so far as to promise to offer you his name if you wished to leave the theater; but he needed to at least be able to lay at your knees the homage of his heart, if not his fortune; but you have enough for two, as everyone knows, and as does he.

MARCELLI: Wretch! . . .

FABIO: Let him finish.

MAZETTO: The delicate nature of his motive led me to help him out. As a theater valet, it was easy for me to put his letters on your dressing table. The first ones were burnt; the following ones, left open, were better received. The last one persuaded you to grant Seigneur Marcelli an appointment, who compensated me quite well! . . .

MARCELLI: Who asked you for this whole story?

FABIO: And me, villain! You hypocrite! How did you serve me? Did you deliver my letters? Who was that veiled woman you sent to me this afternoon, and whom you told me was Signora Corilla?

MAZETTO: Ah, gentlemen, what would you say of me and what would the lady think of me if I had delivered letters written by two different hands and bouquets from two different lovers? Order is needed, and I respect madame too much to have assumed her capable of entertaining two love affairs at the same time. Yet Seigneur Fabio's despair, after my first refusal to serve him, moved me. I let him first give vent to his passion in letters and sonnets, which I pretended to deliver to the signora, assuming that his love could well be that of those who come so often to burn their wings in the flames of the footlights; those passions of schoolboys and poets, which we so often see . . . But it was more serious than that, for Fabio exhausted his purse to sway my virtuous resolution . . .

MARCELLI: That's enough! Signora, these ramblings don't concern us, do they?

CORILLA: Let him speak; we are in no hurry, sir.

MAZETTO: In short, I imagined that Seigneur Fabio's love stopped at his eyes, and since he had never managed to approach madame and had never heard her voice save in music, it would be enough to provide him the satisfaction of an encounter with some creature of the same height and appearance as Signora Corilla . . . I should mention that I had already noticed a little flower girl who sells her flowers along via Toledo or in front of the cafés of Piazza del Molo. She sometimes stops for a moment and sings light-hearted Spanish songs with a very clear tone . . .

MARCELLI: A flower girl who resembles signora; come now! Wouldn't I have noticed her as well?

MAZETTO: Seigneur, she has only recently arrived by Sicilian galleon and still wears the costume of her country.

CORILLA: This is highly unlikely.

MAZETTO: Ask Seigneur Fabio whether the costume didn't lead him to think he saw madame herself pass by earlier?

FABIO: Well, that woman . . .

MAZETTO: That woman, seigneur, is the one waiting for you at the Villa Reale, or rather, who is no longer waiting for you, as the hour has long since passed.

FABIO: Can one imagine a darker, more complicated plot?

MARCELLI: But no; the whole affair is amusing. And look, signora herself can't help but laugh . . . Come, my good man, let us part without bitterness, and give this rascal a good thrashing for me . . . Or rather, look, profit from his idea: the thick cloud which embraced Ixion was for him as good as the divinity whose image it was, and I believe you to be enough of a poet to care little enough for reality.—Good evening, Seigneur Fabio!

FABIO, MAZETTO

FABIO, *to himself*: She was there, and not a word of pity, not a look of interest! She witnessed, coldly and gloomily, this discussion which made me look ridiculous, and she left disdainfully without saying a word, just laughing, no doubt, at my blunder and my simplicity! . . . Oh, you can go, you poor inventive devil, I curse only my bad star. I'm going to dream of my misfortune along the sea, for I no longer have the energy for fury.

MAZETTO: Seigneur, you would do well to go dreaming in the direction of the Villa Réale. The flower girl might still be waiting for you . . .

FABIO, *alone.*

The fact is, I would be interested in meeting this creature and dealing with her in the way she deserves. What woman would consent to such a deed? Is she a simple child who was told how to act, or some brazen girl one had only to pay and then put into action? It takes the soul of a commonplace valet to have judged me able to take the bait even for a moment. And yet she resembles the one I love . . . and when I met her veiled, I thought I recognized her gait and the pure sound of her voice . . . Let's go, it will soon be six o'clock, the last strollers are heading for St. Lucie and Chiaia, and the terraces are filling up with people . . . At this hour, Marcelli is supping happily with his easy conquest. Women only love such heartless libertines.

FABIO, A FLOWER GIRL

FABIO: What do you want of me, little one?

THE FLOWER GIRL: Seigneur, I am selling roses, I am selling spring flowers. Would you like to buy what I have left to decorate your lover's room? They're going to close the garden soon, and I can't bring these back to my father; I'd be beaten. Take them all for three carlinos.

FABIO: Do you really think that someone is awaiting me this evening; do I look like a lucky lover?

THE FLOWER GIRL: Come here into the light. You seem like a handsome gentleman, and if no one's waiting for you, it's because you're waiting . . . Oh, my God!

FABIO: What's the matter, little one? But really, this face . . . Ah, now I understand: you're the false Corilla! . . . At your age, my child, you're off to a bad start!

THE FLOWER GIRL: I'm in truth an honest girl, sir, and you'll come to think better of me. I was disguised as a fine lady, they had me memorize some words; but when I saw that it was all to fool an honest gentleman, I escaped and donned my poor girl's clothing again, and I went, as I do every evening, to sell my flowers on piazza del Molo and along the paths of the Royal Garden.

FABIO: Is this really true?

THE FLOWER GIRL: It is, and I'll bid you good night, sir; since you don't want my flowers, I'll throw them into the sea along the way: tomorrow they'll have faded.

FABIO: Poor girl, these clothes suit you better than the others; my advice is to keep them. You are the wildflower of the fields; but who could confuse the two of you? You do remind me of some of her features, and your heart may be worth more than hers. But who can replace in a lover's soul the beautiful image it takes pleasure in adorning each day with new prestige? That one no longer exists in this earthly reality; it is engraved only in the depths of the loyal heart, and no portrait can ever render its undying beauty.

THE FLOWER GIRL: Yet I've been told that I'm her equal, and with no false modesty, I think that dressed like Signora Corilla, by candlelight, with the aid of the stage and the music, I could please you as much as she, and please you without pearl white and carmine.

FABIO: If your vanity takes offense, little girl, you'll take away even the pleasure I find in looking at you. But you forget that she is the pearl of Spain and Italy, that her foot is the finest and her hand the most royal in the world. Poor child! Poverty is not the culture best suited to such accomplished beauties, who are cared for by luxury and art in turn.

THE FLOWER GIRL: Look at my foot on this marble bench; it is outlined rather nicely in its brown shoe. And have you even touched my hand?

FABIO: True, your foot is charming, and your hand . . . Heavens, how soft it is! . . . But listen, I have no wish to deceive you, my child, it is her alone that I love, and the charm that has seduced me is not born in an evening. For the three months I have been in Naples, I have not missed seeing her a single day at the opera. Too poor to shine next to her, like all the handsome gentlemen who encircle her on her walks, having neither the genius of musicians, nor the renown of the poets who inspire her and who serve her in her talent, I went without hope to intoxicate myself with her presence and her songs, and to take part in this pleasure that belongs to everyone, which for me alone was happiness and life. Oh, you are perhaps indeed her equal . . . but have you that divine grace which reveals itself in so many ways? Have you those tears and that smile? Have you that divine song, without which a divinity is merely a beautiful idol? If so, you would be in her place, and you would not be selling flowers to passersby along Villa Reale . . .

THE FLOWER GIRL: Why would nature have given me her appearance and not her voice? I sing very well, but it would never occur to the directors of San Carlo to gather up a prima donna from the public square . . . Listen to these opera verses I heard at the little Teatro La Fenice. *(She sings.)*

ITALIAN AIR

How sweet it is to have a heart at peace and a calm mind.
Wise it is to love in the summer of life; wiser still to not love at all.

FABIO, *falling to her feet*: Oh, madame, who would not recognize you now? But this cannot be . . . You are a veritable goddess, and you are going to take to the sky! My God, what have I to say to so many gifts? I am unworthy of loving you for not having recognized you right away!

CORILLA: I am no longer the flower girl, then? . . . Well, I thank you; I studied a new role this evening, and you did an admirable job giving me your lines.

FABIO: And Marcelli?

CORILLA: Isn't that him wandering sadly along these bowers, as you were doing a little earlier?

FABIO: Let's take one of these paths and avoid him.

CORILLA: He has seen us, he's coming over.

MARCELLI: So, Seigneur Fabio, you found the flower girl? Well, you have done well, and you're happier than I am this evening.

FABIO: What have you done with Signora Corilla? You were to dine together this evening.

MARCELLI: Well, who can understand a woman's whims? She said she felt unwell, and I was only able to escort her back home; but tomorrow . . .

FABIO: Tomorrow is not this evening, Seigneur Marcelli.

MARCELLI: Let us see this resemblance I've heard so much about . . . Well, she isn't bad! . . . but what of it: no distinction, no grace. Off with you, indulge in your illusions . . . My thoughts are with the prima donna of San Carlo, whom I shall marry a week from now.

CORILLA, *taking on her natural tone of voice*: That will need some thinking over, Seigneur Marcelli. I am in no hurry to make a commitment. I have wealth, I wish to choose. Forgive me for having been an actress as much in love as in the theater, and of having put you both to the test. But I must confess, I'm not sure either of you loves me, and I need to get to know you both better. Seigneur Fabio may only adore the actress in me, and his love requires distance and the lit footlights; and you, Seigneur Marcelli, you appear to love yourself more than anyone else, and your heart doesn't easily rise to the occasion. You are too worldly, and he too much the poet. And now, why don't both of you accompany me. Each of you had wagered to sup with me and I promised to do so with each of you; we will sup together; and Mazetto will serve us.

MAZETTO, *appearing and addressing the audience*: On that note, gentlemen, you see that this improper affair will conclude in a most moral manner.—Forgive the author's faults.[45]

THIRD CASTLE

Castle of cards,[46] castle of Bohemia, castle in Spain—such are the first stations every poet must pass through. Like that famous king Charles Nodier told of, we gain possession of at least seven of them throughout the course of our wandering life—and few among us reach that famous castle of brick and stone, dreamed of in youth—from which some long-haired beauty smiles amorously at us from the only open window, as others reflect the splendors of the evening behind their trellises.

While waiting, I believe that I once passed through the devil's castle. My Cydalise, lost to me, forever lost! . . . A long story, which reached a denouement in a northern country—and which resembles so many others! I only wish to provide here the motif for the following verses, composed in fever and insomnia. This begins in despair and ends in resignation.

Then a pure breeze from early youth returns, and some poetic flowers reopen in the form of the beloved odelette—on the bouncing rhythm of an opera orchestra.

MYSTICISM

LE CHRIST AUX OLIVIERS

Dieu est mort! le ciel est vide . . .
Pleurez! enfants, vous n'avez plus de père

JEAN PAUL

I

Quand le Seigneur, levant au ciel ses maigres bras,
Sous les arbres sacrés, comme font les poètes,
Se fut longtemps perdu dans ses douleurs muettes,
Et se jugea trahi par des amis ingrats,

Il se tourna vers ceux qui l'attendaient en bas
Rêvant d'être des rois, des sages, des prophètes . . .
Mais engourdis, perdus dans le sommeil des bêtes,
Et se prit à crier: «Non, Dieu n'existe pas!»

Ils dormaient. «Mes amis, savez-vous *la nouvelle*?
J'ai touché de mon front à la voûte éternelle;
Je suis sanglant, brisé, souffrant pour bien des jours!»

«Frères, je vous trompais: Abîme! abîme! abîme!
Le dieu manque à l'autel où je suis la victime . . .
Dieu n'est pas! Dieu n'est plus!» Mais ils dormaient toujours!

CHRIST IN THE OLIVE GROVE

God is dead! heaven is empty . . .
Weep, children! You no longer have a father!
JEAN PAUL

I

When the Lord, his frail arms raised to the sky, forlorn,
As poets tend to do, under the sacred trees,
Had long since drunk his mute sorrows down to their lees,
And regarding himself by ungrateful friends scorned,

He turned to those below, those waiting in his midst,
Dreaming of being kings, wise men, prophets, and priests . . .
But slow witted and lost in the slumber of beasts,
And he began to shout: "No, God does not exist!"

They were asleep. "My friends, have you not heard the *news*?
The eternal vault on my brow has placed a bruise;
I am bloody, broken, and for days I have wept!"

"Brothers, I deceived you: Abyss! Abyss! Abyss!
I, the altar's victim, say that god is amiss . . .
There is no God! God is no more!" But still they slept!

II

Il reprit: «Tout est mort! J'ai parcouru les mondes;
Et j'ai perdu mon vol dans leurs chemins lactés,
Aussi loin que la vie, en ses veines fécondes,
Répand des sables d'or et des flots argentés:

Partout le sol désert côtoyé par des ondes,
Des tourbillons confus d'océans agités . . .
Un souffle vague émeut les sphères vagabondes,
Mais nul esprit n'existe en ces immensités.

En cherchant l'œil de Dieu, je n'ai vu qu'une orbite
Vaste, noire et sans fond, d'où la nuit qui l'habite
Rayonne sur le monde et s'épaissit toujours;

Un arc-en-ciel étrange entoure ce puits sombre,
Seuil de l'ancien chaos dont le néant est l'ombre,
Spirale engloutissant les Mondes et les Jours!»

II

He resumed: "All is dead! I have traveled the worlds;
And I have lost my flight within their milky ways,
To where life, through all its veins fertile and unfurled,
Spreads its golden deserts and its silvery waves.

"Where the sandy soil bordered by tides appears,
The turbulent whirlpools of many restless seas . . .
A vague breath from somewhere stirs the wandering spheres,
But no spirit exists in those immensities.

"I sought the eye of God, and saw but a socket,
Vast, black, and bottomless; with naught but night in it,
Deepening and casting on the world its black rays;

"A singular rainbow encircles this dark well,
Threshold of the chaos in which all shadows dwell,
A spiral engulfing all the Worlds and the Days!"

III

«Immobile Destin, muette sentinelle,
Froide Nécessité! . . . Hasard qui, t'avançant
Parmi les mondes morts sous la neige éternelle,
Refroidis, par degrés, l'univers pâlissant,

Sais-tu ce que tu fais, puissance originelle,
De tes soleils éteints, l'un contre l'autre se froissant . . .
Es-tu sûr de transmettre une haleine immortelle,
Entre un monde qui meurt et l'autre renaissant? . . .

O mon père! est-ce toi que je sens en moi-même?
As-tu pouvoir de vivre et de vaincre la mort?
Aurais-tu succombé sous un dernier effort

De cet ange des nuits que frappa l'anathème?
Car je me sens tout seul à pleurer et souffrir,
Hélas! et, si je meurs, c'est que tout va mourir!»

III

"Unmoving Destiny, sentinel most silent,
Cold Necessity! . . . Chance that, starting to traverse
Dead worlds which lie in an endless snowy climate,
Cools, degree by degree, the paling universe,

"Primordial power, what is it that you do,
With your extinguished suns, crumpling together . . .
Is it an immortal breath that you transmit through
Worlds reborn and dying, the two tightly tethered? . . .

"O father! Is it you in me, personalized?
Have you the strength to live and also conquer death?
Or could you have succumbed with your very last breath

"To that angel of nights once anathematized? . . .
For I feel all alone as I suffer and cry,
And if I must perish, it's because all must die!"

IV

Nul n'entendait gémir l'éternelle victime,
Livrant au monde en vain tout son cœur épanché;
Mais prêt à défaillir et sans force penché,
Il appela le *seul*—éveillé dans Solyme:

«Judas! lui cria-t-il, tu sais ce qu'on m'estime,
Hâte-toi de me vendre, et finis ce marché:
Je suis souffrant, ami! sur la terre couché . . .
Viens! ô toi qui, du moins, as la force du crime!»

Mais Judas s'en allait, mécontent et pensif,
Se trouvant mal payé, plein d'un remords si vif
Qu'il lisait ses noirceurs sur tous les murs écrites . . .

Enfin Pilate seul, qui veillait pour César,
Sentant quelque pitié, se tourna par hasard:
«Allez chercher ce fou!» dit-il aux satellites.»

IV

But no one had heard the eternal victim moan,
Giving up to the world his vented heart in vain;
And ready to faint and feeling weak and in pain,
He called out to the *one* in Solyma,[47] alone:

"Judas! You know my worth," he cried out, "it is time!
Come and finish this deal, make haste and sell me, friend:
I'm suffering, Judas! My strength is at an end.
Come! O you who, at least, wield the power of crime!"

But Judas went his way, discontent and pensive,
Badly paid, full of a remorse so extensive
That he read his black deeds written on every wall . . .

Pilate alone, Caesar's prefect in the city,
Turned to the satellites,[48] though feeling some pity:
"Go, seek out this madman!" was his reluctant call.

V

C'était bien lui, ce fou, cet insensé sublime . . .
Cet Icare oublié qui remontait les cieux,
Ce Phaéton perdu sous la foudre des dieux,
Ce bel Atys meurtri que Cybèle ranime!

L'augure interrogeait le flanc de la victime,
La terre s'enivrait de ce sang précieux . . .
L'univers étourdi penchait sur ses essieux,
Et l'Olympe un instant chancela vers l'abîme.

«Réponds! criait César à Jupiter Ammon,
Quel est ce nouveau dieu qu'on impose à la terre?
Et si ce n'est un dieu, c'est au moins un démon . . . »

Mais l'oracle invoqué pour jamais dut se taire;
Un seul pouvait au monde expliquer ce mystère:
—Celui qui donna l'âme aux enfants du limon.

V

That sublime lunatic, his faculties plundered . . .
That wayward Icarus, again climbing the skies,
It was that Phaethon[49] lost to the godly thunder,
Handsome, murdered Atys whom Cybele revives![50]

The augur examined the side of the victim,
The earth grew drunk on the dear blood of the one shunned . . .
And the universe reeled upon its axles, stunned,
As Olympus tottered to the void from its rim.

"Answer!" Caesar cried out to Jupiter Ammon,[51]
"What's this new god imposed on the earth here today?
And if it's not a god, it's at least a demon . . ."

But the oracle called had to remain silent;
One alone could explain what this mystery meant:
—He who had given soul to the children of clay.

DAPHNÉ

Jam redit et virgo . . .

La connais-tu, Dafné, cette ancienne romance,
Au pied du sycomore, ou sous les lauriers blancs,
Sous l'olivier, le myrte, ou sous les saules tremblants,
Cette chanson d'amour qui toujours recommence? . . .

Reconnais-tu le Temple au péristyle immense,
Et les citrons amers ou s'imprimaient tes dents,
Et la grotte, fatale aux hôtes imprudents,
Où du dragon vaincu dort l'antique semence? . . .

Ils reviendront, ces Dieux que tu pleures toujours!
Le temps va ramener l'ordre des anciens jours;
La terre a tressailli d'un souffle prophétique . . .

Cependant la sibylle au visage latin
Est endormie encor sous l'arc de Constantin
—Et rien n'a dérangé le sévère portique.

DAPHNE

Jam redit et virgo . . .[52]

That old love song, Daphne,[53] is it one that you knew?
By the sycamore tree, or by the white laurels,
The olive tree, myrtle, or quivering willows,
That eternal love song, which always starts anew! . . .

Remember the Temple with the long peristyle,
And the bitter lemons into which your teeth pressed,[54]
And that grotto, fatal to the foolhardy guest,
Where the vanquished dragon's ancient seed sleeps the while? . . .

They will return to us, those Gods for whom you weep!
Time will revive the ways of the old days that sleep,
A breath of prophecy makes the earth shake below . . .

Yet the sibyl with the Latin visage, serene,
Is sleeping still beneath the arch of Constantine
—And nothing has disturbed the severe Portico.

VERS DORÉS

Eh quoi! tout est sensible
PYTHAGORE

Homme, libre penseur! te crois-tu seul pensant
Dans ce monde où la vie éclate en toute chose?
Des forces que tu tiens ta liberté dispose,
Mais de tous tes conseils l'univers est absent.

Respecte dans la bête un esprit agissant:
Chaque fleur est une âme à la Nature éclose;
Un mystère d'amour dans le métal repose;
«Tout est sensible!» Et tout sur ton être est puissant.

Crains, dans le mur aveugle, un regard qui t'épie:
A la matière même un verbe est attaché . . .
Ne la fais pas servir à quelque usage impie!

Souvent dans l'être obscur habite un Dieu caché;
Et comme un œil naissant couvert par ses paupières,
Un pur esprit s'accroît sous l'écorce des pierres!

GOLDEN VERSES

What! All is sentient!
PYTHAGORAS

Man, free thinker! Do you believe you think alone
In this world in which life bursts forth from everything?
Your liberty employs the strength you have within
But the world is absent from everything you own.

Respect in every beast a spirit that is true:
Souls blossom in Nature, in each flower petal;
A mystery of love lies sleeping in metal;
For "all is sentient!" And all will impact you.

Beware in the blind wall the gaze spying on you:
In the heart of matter itself, a verb resides . . .
Take care not to put it to some impious use!

Often in dark being there lives a God that hides;
And like the nascent eye under its lids, unshown,
So does a pure spirit grow underneath the stone!

RUE DE LAVIELLE LANTERNE

LYRICISM

ESPAGNE

Mon doux pays des Espagnes
Qui voudrait fuir ton beau ciel,
Tes cités et tes montagnes,
Et ton printemps éternel?

Ton air pur qui nous enivre,
Tes jours moins beaux que tes nuits,
Tes champs, où Dieu voudrait vivre
S'il quittait son paradis?

Autrefois, ta souveraine,
L'Arabie, en te fuyant,
Laissa sur ton front de reine
Sa couronne d'Orient!

Un écho redit encore
A ton rivage enchanté
L'antique refrain du Maure:
Gloire, amour et liberté!

SPAIN

My dear, sweet country of Spain,
Who would flee your lovely skies,
Your cities, your mountain plain,
And your spring that never dies?

Your intoxicating air,
Your days, your lovelier nights,
Your fields, which would be God's lair
Should he leave his paradise?

In the past, your sovereign,
Arabia, when fleeing,
Its crown of the Orient
Left on the brow of your queen!

To your lush, enchanted shore
Comes an echo from above
The old refrain of the Moor:
Glory, liberty, and love!

CHŒUR D'AMOUR

Ici l'on passe
Des jours enchantés!
L'ennui s'efface
Aux cœurs attristés
Comme la trace
Des flots agités.

Heure frivole
Et qu'il faut saisir,
Passion folle
Qui n'est qu'un désir,
Et qui s'envole
Après le plaisir!

Piquillo (avec Dumas)
Musique de Monpou

LOVE CHORUS

One passes here
Most enchanting days!
Sad hearts find cheer
As all worry fades
Like the lone tear
In the restless waves.

Moment in flight
Seize like a treasure,
Wild delight
Beyond all measure,
Then out of sight:
Departing pleasure!

Piquillo (with Dumas)
Music by Monpou

CHANSON GOTHIQUE

Belle épousée,
J'aime tes pleurs!
C'est la rosée
qui sied aux fleurs.

Les belles choses
N'ont qu'un printemps,
Semons de roses
Les pas du Temps!

Soit brune ou blonde,
Faut-il choisir?
Le Dieu du monde,
C'est la Plaisir.

Les Monténégrins
Music de Limnander

GOTHIC SONG

Beautiful bride
I love your tears!
The dew undried
Of flowered years.

Beautiful things
Have but one spring,
The roses climb:
Footsteps of Time!

Brunette or blond
Why must one choose?
Pleasure alone,
Is this world's muse.

The Montenegrins
Music by Limnander

LA SÉRÉNADE

(imitée d'Uhland)

—Oh! quel doux chant m'éveille?
—Près de ton lit je veille,
Ma fille! et n'entends rien . . .
Rendors-toi, c'est chimère!
—J'entends dehors, ma mère,
Un chœur aérien! . . .

—Ta fièvre va renaître.
—Ces chants de la fenêtre
Semblent s'être approchés.
—Dors, pauvre enfant malade,
Qui rêves sérénade . . .
Les galants sont couchés!

—Les hommes! que m'importe?
Un nuage m'emporte . . .
Adieu le monde, adieu!
Mère, ces sons étranges
C'est le concert des anges
Qui m'appellent à Dieu!

Musique du prince Poniatowski

THE SERENADE

(imitated from Uhland)

Oh! what is that sweet song?
—I've been here all night long,
My girl, and hear nothing . . .
A dream, nothing to fear!
—Yet mother, I can hear
A lovely choir sing! . . .

—You'll make your fever grow.
—These songs at the window
Seem to be drawing near.
—Sleep, child, I'm afraid
You dream a serenade . . .
The suitors sleep, my dear!

—Men, they're of no import . . .
A cloud's paying me court . . .
These sounds that are so odd . . .
Farewell, old world, farewell!
A concert of angels
Is calling me to God![55]

Music by Prince Poniatowski

TRANSLATOR'S NOTES

1. *Il pastor fido* (*The Faithful Shepherd*), a work by Giovanni Battista Guarini (1539–1612), was first performed in 1585 and first published in 1590. This citation comes from a monologue by the character Mirtillo in Act III, scene I: "O gentle spring, youth of the newborn year, / Mother of flowers / new verdure, and new loves . . ."
2. This friend was French novelist, dramatist, poet, and art critic, Arsène Houssaye (1815–1896).
3. From a poem by Houssaye that underwent several titles: initially "Les Belles Amoureuses," then "Le Beau Temps des poètes," and finally, "Vingt ans" (Twenty years), the title to which Nerval later refers. Houssaye published these quatrains in *l'Artiste*, following a note on Nerval, who had just had a mental breakdown.
4. The "Street of the Deanery." The demolition of this quarter began in 1851.
5. "Both Arcadians"—a citation from Virgil's *Eclogues*, VII, V, 4.
6. Camille Rogier (1810–1896), painter and illustrator.
7. Nerval's lifelong friend, the poet, critic, and dramatist Théophile Gautier (1811–1872). Although a significant French poet and writer of his time, he is better remembered today for originating the phrase "Art for art's sake" and as being the dedicatee of Baudelaire's *Les fleurs du mal*.
8. Cydalise I was Rogier's mistress, and Victorine was a longtime mistress of Gautier. Sarah the blonde alludes to Victor Hugo's poem, "Sara la baigneuse" (Sara the bather) from *Les Orientales*.
9. Also from Houssaye's aforementioned poem "Vingt ans."
10. Jeanne-Sylvanie-Sophie Plessy (1819–1897) began her career at the Comedie Française at the age of sixteen.

11. A play written by Nerval, which he adapted from Paul Scarron.
12. Édouard Ourliac (1813–1848), a journalist, novelist, and actor.
13. Célestin Nanteuil (1813–1873), a painter and illustrator with close ties to the French Romantics.
14. Charles Émile Wattier (1800–1868), a French painter who was influenced by François Boucher and Jean-Antoine Watteau.
15. Auguste de Châtillon (1808–1881), French painter and sculptor, and friend of Victor Hugo.
16. Théodore Chassériau (1819–1856), a French Romantic painter and a student of Ingres who later fell under the influence of Delacroix. The overmantels of which Nerval speaks belonged at the beginning of the twentieth century to Maurice Barrès and Jacques-Émile Blanche. Their whereabouts are currently unknown.
17. Alcide Joseph Lorentz (1813–1891), painter.
18. Théodore Rousseau (1812–1867), a French painter of the Barbizon school.
19. Alphonse Karr (1809–1890) was a journalist, humorist, and a friend of Nerval.
20. Sulpice Guillaume Chevalier, known as Gavarni (1804–1866), was a French illustrator.
21. The sonnet in question was published untitled in *L'Abeille* in December 1835 and later collected in Gautier's collection *La Comédie de la Mort* (1838).
22. Théophile de Viau (1590–1626) was a French Baroque poet and dramatist who authored *La Maison de Sylvie*, a series of odes concerning the author's love for Sylvie, the Duchesse of Montmorency. "Sylvie" is, of course, the title of Nerval's own classic novella.
23. Nerval is referring to a group of artists and writers known as the "Petit Cénacle," best remembered for their eccentric behavior. Their best-known member, aside from Nerval and Gautier, was Petrus Borel, who went by the moniker of "the Lycanthrope."
24. A parody of the Gospel according to Saint John in which Jesus tells a paralytic to "Get up . . . and walk."
25. Giacomo Meyerbeer's opera *Robert le diable* was one of the first to be performed at the Paris Opéra; it premiered on 21 November 1831.

26. Jules-Claude Ziegler (1804–1856) was a French painter and ceramicist, and a student of Ingres.

27. Nerval is presumably making a pun on the word "vandal."

28. Nerval seems to be confusing his history here: the accident took place on 15 October 1739, whereas Guillaume Dubois died in 1723.

29. The "queen of the sabbath" (*reine du sabbat*) had originally been the "Queen of Sheba" (*Reine de saba*) in an earlier publication of the poem.

30. Mother Saguet's cabaret was a gathering place for literary and artistic personalities.

31. Henry Massé d'Egmont (1810–1863) was the French translator of E. T. A. Hoffmann's stories, published in four volumes in 1836. Roger de Beauvoir (1806–1866) was a young dandy and author of, among other works, *L'Écolier de Cluny, ou Le Sophisme* (1852). Pierre Eugène Giraud (1806–1881) was a French painter well known in his time, now best remembered for his portrait of Gustave Flaubert.

32. Anacreon (ca. 582–ca. 485 BCE) was a Greek lyric poet; Bion of Smyrna was an ancient Greek bucolic poet of the first or second century BCE whose influence was significant but most of whose work has been lost.

33. The *Roman comique*, by Paul Scarron (1610–1660), was one of Nerval's favorite works, and one of the first French novels.

34. *Piqueton*: A watered-down wine that served as a poor man's drink.

35. César-Pierre Richelet (1626–1698), a French grammarian and lexicographer, edited a seventeenth-century rhyming dictionary.

36. This poem is an adaptation of a prose translation Nerval made of a sonnet by Gottfried August Bürger (1747–1794).

37. Nerval's translation casts a melancholic tone not to be found in the Greek.

38. The *proverbe dramatique* was a high-society theatrical genre in the late eighteenth century usually associated with Louis Carrogis Carmontelle. It consisted of a single scene that would illustrate a well-known proverb, which the audience would try to guess at the end.

39. Jupiter possessed and impregnated Danaë by transforming himself into a shower of gold: Fabio still suspects that his presents alone have procured him a rendezvous.

40. Pietro Metastasio (1698–1782), Italian poet and librettist.

41. Giovanni Paisiello (1740–1816) was an Italian musician who wrote a *Barber of Seville* (1782) that rivaled Rossini's version in popularity. Domenico Cimarosa (1749–1801) was his rival.
42. The painting in question (completed in 1610), although once attributed to Caravaggio, is by Artemisia Gentileschi (1593–1656).
43. A knight heroine in several operas and works, but most famously in Ariosto's *Orlando Furioso*.
44. A character from Jean de La Fontaine's fable, "Daphnis et Alcimadure," which would inspire the opera of the same name by Jean-Joseph Cassanéa de Mondonville.
45. All Spanish plays used to end with this phrase.
46. *Château de cartes*: what in English is referred to as a "house" of cards.
47. Solyma was the Roman name for Jerusalem.
48. "Satellites" here is in a military, not astronomical, sense.
49. Son of Apollo, punished for almost destroying the world with his father's chariot.
50. Cybele (goddess of the earth) punished Atys, a Phyigian shepherd, for not returning her love; stricken with madness, he emasculated himself. He is supposedly resuscitated each spring, which links him to the Egyptian god, Osiris. In "Isis," Nerval traces Cybele's name changes into that of her "true" name, Isis.
51. Jupiter is the king of the gods in Olympus, Ammon the Greek god of the sun: the Greeks and the Romans identified the two as one.
52. From Virgil's *Eclogues*: "Now the virgin returns . . ." Implying, for the Romans, the return of the Golden Age.
53. Daphne was a nymph who had herself changed into a laurel to escape Apollo's unwanted attention.
54. An echo of the titular character performing the same action in Nerval's story "Octavie."
55. This is Nerval's adaptation/translation of a poem by German poet Ludwig Uhland (1787–1862), "Das Ständchen," from his short cycle of poems *Sterbeklänge* (Death sounds). To maintain Nerval's choices in rendering the poem into French song, this English translation is thus a translation of a translation.

ILLUSTRATIONS

Napoleon Jeffries has translated the work of Pierre Mac Orlan and Honoré de Balzac.